Travel to Maurice's World!

Maurice's World is your passport to adventure—online. Explore other books in the *Maurice's Valises* series. Make friends from all over the world. Earn moral badges and collect treasures from Maurice's travels. Create your own Moral Scrolls and play fun games. Plus, stamp your virtual passport, using the special code below. And there's more to come soon, including a valise hunt!

YOUR SPECIAL CODE
IS **WOLF**

The Books Before...

In the Beginning
In the first book, Maurice, an orphan mouse, travels to
New Zealand, where he is visited by the Muse of Mice,
is given a great responsibility, and Maurice learns the value
of always telling the truth.

The Micetro of Moscow

In the second book, Maurice travels to Russia, where he befriends a musical (yet unpopular) mouse, Henry, who helps Tchaikovsky finish *Swan Lake*. Maurice learns that everyone is special in his or her own way.

Casablanca

In the third book, Maurice's adventures take him to Morocco, where a selfless act allows him to befriend a bespectacled camel, Cecil, and learn the true meaning of friendship.

MOUSE PRINTS PRESS
Prinsengracht 1053-S Boot
1017 JE Amsterdam Netherlands

Maurice's Valises

Moral Tails in an Immoral World

Medicine Mouse

By J. S. Friedman

Illustrations by Chris Beatrice

"Come in, come in. Take a seat anywhere," invited the elderly mouse as he let in the last group of snow-covered guests.

"Call me Maurice," he said, shuffling back to the fire crackling in the fireplace—or, more exactly, to his special storytelling chair, which just happened to be near the fire crackling in the fireplace.

"Call me Molly," said a young voice from the kitchen.

"And call me Mya," mimicked a second voice amid a loud sound of crashing pots and pans.

"And call me Marigold," giggled a tiny third voice as all three girls, Maurice's nieces, popped their heads around the kitchen doorway.

Grandpa Maurice smiled at the kitchen chorus and sat down. He adjusted his warm winter story-telling scarf (unlike his summer one) and surveyed his ninety-eight grandmice, plus old friends and new ones.

All were cozy in his living room—deep in in the woods, in the base of an old sycamore tree—away from the uncozy wind and snow outside.

Since everyone had come to hear Maurice tell one of his stories, Maurice began to sort through the traveling-tale file in his head.

Before he could find just the right tale, impatient Rufus, a little neighborhood mouse squeaked, "Can you tell us the teepee story?"

"Ha! That's just what I was about choose," exclaimed Maurice.

PAW NOTE

A conical-shaped tent made of long sticks and buffalo hides, used by many Native Americans.

"Let me find that valise." Maurice got up and turned to the towering stack of old valises behind him.

Each valise had a label and lots of stickers from wherever Maurice had traveled with it.

Unfortunately, the one he was looking for was on the bottom. And when he tugged it, they all came tumbling down.

This created a cloud of dust so thick the mice could barely see Maurice, but they could hear him: "Aaaachoo!"

When the dust finally settled, there stood Maurice, holding just the valise he wanted.

He dusted himself off.
He dusted the valise off.
Then, he opened it.

Out came one necklace of beads, one
feathered headband, and, of course, one
Moral Scroll.

PAW NOTE

*A paper with a wise saying written on it. The saying is the lesson
learned from a particular traveling tale.*

Maurice put on the headband, adjusted its feathers and, settled back into his chair.

"Well, years ago," he began, "I traveled many days on a tall ship, sailing from the other side of the ocean.

"I had a funny experience my very first night at sea. I woke up to see a mouse, upside down, staring into my face.

"'Hello,' I said, 'I'm Maurice of the Valise.'

"'Hello to you,' said the upside-down mouse. 'I'm Basil the bat—see?' And with that, he spread his wings.

"'I want to let you know to be careful. There are rats on board, and they steal.'

13

"I immediately checked my valise, and guess what?
My food was already gone."

"Maurice," said Rufus, interrupting, "you were robbed?
Were you very mad?"

"Shhhhhush, Rufus. Ok, well, at first I was annoyed. But
being mad wouldn't get my food back. It wouldn't help.

"So I chose to be happy that at least I was warned. That's what I chose to do.

"So, where was I? Oh yes, Basil flew off, and I went back to bed.

"In the morning, right side up, was a small bag of food beside me. And there above me, hanging upside down, was Basil, settling in to sleep for the day.

"Weeks later, Basil told me we were getting close to land.

"He had flown over the sea at night and had heard the sounds of the port. You see, as a bat, Basil couldn't see. But he could hear—really hear.

"And what he heard made him warn me again to be careful when we reached the harbor.

"When I came ashore, I was in a big, busy port on the Eastern coast.

"I had come here, to America, because I was told the streets were paved with cheese!

"But I looked around and didn't see any cheese.

"All I saw were cobblestones.

"And, then, to my horror, I saw a hungry-looking cat eyeing me from behind a barrel.

"I froze.

"Then I heard the always-welcome, always-protective voice of the Muse of Mice say: 'Go West, young mouse—wisdom awaits you. Go West. NOW!'

"I grabbed my valise (this very one) and ran as fast as my little legs could take me.

"I spotted an old horse standing in front of a wagon, munching his food. I ran up his leg and jumped into his feed bucket, just as that cat raced by, looking for me."

"And weren't you really, really mad that the cat chased you?" interrupted Rufus again.

Shush, Rufus. Be patient—I'll tell you later.

"So I introduced myself to the horse: 'My name is Maurice.'

"'Hi. I'm Higgenbottom. Just having a bit of supper. Care to share a little grain with me? Just don't eat too much. I have a long journey tomorrow. I'm pulling this wagon West,' he snorted..

"'I'm going West too, but which way is West?'

"'Ride with me and see for yourself,' invited Higgenbottom.

"Which is exactly what I did.

"The next day, and many days after that, we bumped along roads, crossed streams, and drove through deep valleys.

"Finally, we arrived at Higgenbottom's West. We had reached the prairies, where all you could see was grass and sky.

"At night, Higgenbottom told stories about the Native Americans, who lived here in teepees made of long sticks and buffalo hides.

"And he spoke of buffalo who were like big, furry cows.

"He said that if a large group started to run, the ground would rumble like thunder under them.

"I knew it would hurt my new friend Higgenbottom's feelings to tell him, but when he slept, he snored. And his snores rumbled like thunder, too.

"But I kept this to myself.

"One morning, after many weeks of travel, I heard rumbling. It wasn't Higgenbottom.

"It was a rumbling cloud of dust that was getting closer. And closer. And closer, until the cloud became a crowd of buffalo racing around us.

"My valise and I flew out of the feed bucket as Higgenbottom and the wagon galloped away with the buffalo, leaving me behind."

"And weren't you really, really, really mad?" interrupted Rufus for the third time.

"Hush, hush, and again, hush," said Maurice with a grin. "Not mad, just surprised. And Higgenbottom didn't really choose to leave me—he just got carried away.

"Well, when I fell, I fell, unhurt, onto the head of Pip, a prairie dog who was hiding in his hole.

"'Well, this is odd. . . .' exclaimed Pip with a yip. 'A mouse fell on my head! Or flew there! What a day. What. A. Day.

"'First the rumbling on my roof. Now this. I must speak with Mordaci the Medicine Mouse. He's wise. He'll explain it.'

"With that, Pip grabbed me, I grabbed my valise and off we went.

PAW NOTE

A small, burrowing animal, native to the prairies of North America.

"Now, Pip lived in a prairie-dog town called Yipee, with lots of holes, lots of tunnels, and lots of prairie dogs.

"And Mordaci the Medicine Mouse lived in a teepee, not too far from Yipee.

"But the trip took forever, because prairie dogs may not pass other prairie dogs without stopping to greet each other.

"So we made hundreds of bows. We said hundreds of 'hellos.'

"And Pip explained hundreds of times: 'I am off to see Mordaci the Medicine Mouse with my new friend, Maurice, the flying mouse who fell on my head.'

"It was nighttime before we reached the circle of teepees.

"There, we saw the old Plains Indians Medicine Man, Wisebeyondhisears.

"He wore a big, feathered headdress and sat with some children around a campfire.

"Pip whispered that Mordaci the Medicine Mouse, Wisebeyondhisears's chief adviser, was hidden on the man's head, whispering wise things for him to say.

"We crept closer to hear Wisebeyondhisears:

"'Others steal our land, our food, our way of life. We as a tribe, we as a people, must learn from our struggles.

" 'A struggle is also going on inside me. It is a struggle between two wolves,' said Wiesbeyondhisears. 'One wolf is wicked—he is full of anger, envy, greed, meanness, and lies.

" 'The other wolf is good—he is full of kindness, love, generosity, truth, and understanding.

" 'And every day, the same struggle is going on inside you and inside everybody else.'

"The children thought about this. Then one child asked, 'Which wolf will win?'

" 'The one you feed,' replied Wisebeyondhisears.

PAW NOTE

Legend built from another tribe's fable, "Two Wolves, a Cherokee Legend."

"What does that mean?" interrupted Rufus for the fourth time, not being able to withhold his excitement.

"Shushshsh," said everyone in the den.

"Wisebeyondhisears waited as the children thought about this," continued Maurice.

"Then he got up, smiled, and returned to his teepee. Inside, he took off his feathered headdress and settled down to think.

"Mordaci the Medicine Mouse hopped out of the headdress, wearing his own feathered headband. (I'm wearing it now.)

"He was very old, but he had a twinkle in his eyes.

"We immediately greeted, as many mice do, by touching noses. But something VERY strange happened!

"A shock went right through my nose and into my body. In that instant, all of Mordaci's wisdom and experiences were transferred into me!!!!

"Mordaci jumped back and looked at me. 'Aha!' he cried. 'So you have come. You are a special mouse, too! In all my years, I have never met another special mouse. This is remarkable. Remarkable!

'But it has been foretold by the Muse of Mice that when two special mice should meet, the one with the most knowledge must share.

'I have lived a long, long time and learned many things. Now my learnings are yours to share with others.

"'This is indeed a special day—or should I say, night? Please take this necklace of beads and this feather headdress to remember me by.'

"Then Mordaci the Medicine Mouse removed his feathered headdress, and what do you know?

"The great, wise medicine mouse had enormous ears just like mine!

"Pip—who had been waiting patiently to ask Mordaci to explain why I, Maurice, the flying mouse, had fallen on his head—now understood.

"He couldn't wait to get back home to tell his hundreds of friends how, that day, a little bit of wisdom had fallen on his head. The end," sighed Grandpa Maurice.

He looked at all his listeners. He looked at Rufus, who was about to interrupt again.

"Now, Rufus, 'later' is now, and for your information, I was never, ever mad. I've always fed the other wolf."

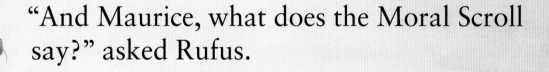

"And Maurice, what does the Moral Scroll say?" asked Rufus.

"OK, I'll tell you now," said Maurice, carefully unscrolling the scroll. Once it was open, he turned it for all to see as he read:

We all have struggles
and choices in our lives.
It is up to us to think
and choose wisely

At first, there were whispers as Maurice rerolled the Moral Scroll and put it in his lap. Then the room got quiet with the sound of a lot of thinking.

Soon, though, Rufus thought of one more question to ask Maurice, so he asked, "What do you feed a wolf?"

But Maurice didn't answer.

True to form, Maurice was already sleeping peacefully in his comfy chair. Like a baby.

And snoring with a rumble. Like Higgenbottom.

The end, again.

And, more to come ...

Myths, legends, and fables were originally very old, spoken stories, handed down from generation to generation to explain how natural phenomena or social customs came to be. Native Americans are thought to have come to North America around 16,500 to 13,000 years ago. Their stories were based on what was natural and observed, and they were designed to teach.

While cultures and customs varied, all Native American Indian beliefs were rooted in Animism, meaning that they believed the universe was bound together by the spirits within all natural life—from plants, animals, humans, water, and even the Earth itself.

From www.IndianLegend.com.

Acknowledgments

My special thanks to Fancy Pants Global in Reykjavik (and Iceland, too), for being Maurice's home away from his forest home. Their diligence and artistry have allowed Maurice not only to grow, but to become a global mouse.

To Stephanie Arnold, for her unwavering support and crucial editorial contributions. To Joe Landry, for his Salzburg friendship and guidance. To Tim Turner, for his steady hand and creative collaboration. To my wife Cheryl, for her support and tolerance for an all-consuming project.

And, of course, to Chris Beatrice, for his illustrations and vision, and for believing that Maurice is a special mouse.